Karen Grimes

A Celebration of the Georgia State Symbols

Karen Grimes

Illustrated by Evelyn Knight and Karen Grimes

MOUNTAIN ARBOR PRESS

MOUNTAIN ARBOR
PRESS
Alpharetta, GA

ISBN: 978-1-63183-301-4

Library of Congress Control Number: 2018943939

Printed in the United States of America   0 6 0 5 1 8

∞ This paper meets the requirements of ANSI/NISO Z39.48-1992 (Permanence of Paper)

Illustrations by Evelyn Knight and Karen Grimes

This book is dedicated to

Mrs. Sandra Deal

in appreciation of her

efforts to further children's literacy

in the state of Georgia.

"Wake up, wake up, Mark! Today is the day we have been waiting for!

We are going to the picnic over by the marsh to see all the Georgia state symbols!" Maggie exclaimed.

Mark is Maggie's little brother, and they are brown thrashers.

Maggie and Mark live in a beautiful azalea bush behind a farmhouse just west of Savannah.

The brown thrasher is the official state bird of Georgia. Brown thrashers have long tails and long, curved beaks. They usually build their nests in bushes, not trees. They enjoy eating fruits, nuts, and sometimes insects. They also love to sing!

The native azalea is the Georgia state wildflower. Native azaleas grow throughout Georgia and bloom in many different colors: pink, red, yellow, and white. Callaway Gardens in Pine Mountain, Georgia, is one of the largest azalea gardens in the world!

Maggie's mom was gathering crunchy acorns for their breakfast under the big live oak tree.

She knew they would need a good breakfast for the big day.

The live oak tree is the state tree of Georgia. Live oak trees mainly grow in the southern part of Georgia and along the coast. They are very large trees, and most range from forty-five to sixty-four feet high. Some of the live oak trees in Georgia are over two hundred years old!

The live oak tree received its name because its leaves stay green year-round and always look beautiful. It also produces acorns that many animals love to eat.

After breakfast, Maggie and Mark went
over to see their friend Bobby.

Bobby is a bobwhite quail that lives in a grassy thicket behind the yard where they live.

The bobwhite quail is the Georgia state game bird. Bobwhite quail have large bodies, short tails, and short, curved beaks. They like to eat insects, fruits, and seeds.

Bobwhite quail like to build their nests close to the ground, usually around tall grasses and weeds. They also use grasses and weeds to build their nests. During the winter months, they live in groups called coveys.

Bobby was so excited about the surprise his grandfather had brought him yesterday. It was a beautiful piece of staurolite.

Staurolite is the Georgia state mineral. It is a mineral known for good luck and is sometimes called a "fairy cross" because you can usually see a cross in the middle. Most staurolite is found in North Georgia.

Maggie was excited
to show Bobby the
amethyst quartz
gemstone she had found
down by the river yesterday
and the shark's tooth Mark had
found in the back field.

Quartz is the Georgia state gem. Some quartz gemstones have a purple color called amethyst, and some have a clear-white color. They form in many different shapes and are fun to find!

The shark's tooth is the Georgia state fossil. Many years ago, the coastal plain area of Georgia was covered by the ocean. It was common for the prehistoric sharks to lose teeth and leave them behind for us to find!

Anna and Dan live in the woods behind Bobby's thicket and were gathering peaches and onions for the picnic.

Anna and Dan are white-tailed deer.

The white-tailed deer is the Georgia state mammal. White-tailed deer have beautiful brown fur with snow-white bellies and chests. Male deer are called "bucks" and have antlers; female deer are called "does" and do not have antlers.

Peaches are the Georgia state fruit. They grow mainly in the middle part of the state. Georgia is sometimes called the "Peach State" because so many peaches are grown in Georgia. Vidalia onions are the Georgia state vegetable. Vidalia onions are only grown in Georgia and are known as the world's sweetest onions!

Maggie and Mark saw Johnny as they passed his burrow. Johnny is a gopher tortoise. Johnny had collected peanuts that he had dug from the back field to take to the picnic.

Harold, a honeybee, was buzzing around an old pine tree.

The gopher tortoise is the Georgia state reptile. Gopher tortoises live in burrows that they dig in the ground, and some can be very deep. They mainly live in the southern part of Georgia.

Peanuts are the Georgia state crop. Peanuts are used to make peanut butter and candy. Many animals like to eat them too. The honeybee is the Georgia state insect. Honeybees are common throughout the state and produce delicious honey.

On the way to the picnic, Maggie saw Betsy, a green tree frog, watching Sammy, a largemouth bass, splashing around in the Savannah River.

The green tree frog is the Georgia state amphibian. Green tree frogs like to live around ponds, rivers, streams, and lakes.

The largemouth bass is the Georgia state fish. Largemouth bass are found in rivers and lakes throughout Georgia. They eat worms, insects, and small fish.

Maggie saw Kate, a tiger swallowtail butterfly, flutter in toward a beautiful Cherokee rose.

The tiger swallowtail is the Georgia state butterfly. Tiger swallowtails are very beautiful and can be seen throughout Georgia.

The Cherokee rose is the Georgia state flower. Cherokee roses grow in all 159 Georgia counties. They bloom in early spring and have many thorns. There are many legends about this beautiful flower! One legend is that everywhere a tear fell during the Trail of Tears, a Cherokee rose bush grew.

Maggie and Mark went down to the beach and arrived just in time to see Mary, a right whale, leaping out of the ocean.

The right whale is the Georgia state marine mammal. Right whales come down from the cold North Atlantic waters and live off the coast of Georgia in the warm ocean waters during the time they give birth.

Abby, a knobbed whelk, was on the beach. The knobbed whelk is the Georgia state seashell. Knobbed whelks are found along the coast of Georgia. They have a beautiful tan, spiral shell with spines on top! Their colors are formed from the minerals found in the coastal waters.

Everyone gathered for the picnic, where they enjoyed peanuts, peaches, and Vidalia onions!

Before everyone started home, they sang "Georgia on My Mind," the Georgia state song. They all had a great day!

The Georgia State Symbols

Georgia State Amphibian	Green Tree Frog
Georgia State Bird	Brown Thrasher
Georgia State Butterfly	Tiger Swallowtail
Georgia State Crop	Peanut
Georgia State Fish	Largemouth Bass
Georgia State Flower	Cherokee Rose
Georgia State Fossil	Shark's Tooth
Georgia State Fruit	Peach
Georgia State Game Bird	Bobwhite Quail
Georgia State Gem	Amethyst Quartz
Georgia State Insect	Honeybee
Georgia State Marine Mammal	Right Whale
Georgia State Mammal	Whitetail Deer
Georgia State Mineral	Staurolite
Georgia State Reptile	Gopher Tortoise
Georgia State Seashell	Knobbed Whelk
Georgia State Song	"Georgia on My Mind"
Georgia State Tree	Live Oak
Georgia State Vegetable	Vidalia Onion
Georgia State Wildflower	Native Azalea

About the Author

Karen Grimes is a resident of Milledgeville, Georgia. She graduated from Florida State University with a degree in education. She recently retired from Georgia Military College Prep School, where she taught Georgia history.